MW00979197

This Book Belongs To:

i was in my garden early one day
When i saw all the fairies come out to play.
They saw me standing with my mouth wide open
Not a word could i have spoken
They gave me a golden feather as a token
So that my memory of our meeting would be unbroken.

Dedicated to all who see what they believe
And to Georgia who talks to Fairies.

i sit here dreaming of the day when all
people laugh and play. When they only
dream of love and peace, i will wake from
this deep deep sleep.

The Secret World of Fairies

Illustrations by Bernard Rosa
Stories by Janine Fuller

NEW HOLLAND

Special Thanks to

Adam Ibrahim	Levi Jones-Leary
Connor Simpson	Matthew Levitt
Danielle Lye	Maui Szasz
Ella Matthews	Nicole Rosa
Georgia Jeffrey	Rozi Komlos
Jehaan Ibrahim	Rozlynn Myers
Jordan Herbert	Sabina Kohary
Joshua Robinson	Sam Levitt
Karissa Kohary	Sienna Clealand-Johnson
Karla Maree Dixon	Tianna Marrie Echegaray
Kata Komlos	Tim Simpson
Kathleen Simpson	Zoe Brock

Make Up
Andrea Komlos
Amber Donnellan

Stories, stylist and costumes
Janine Fuller

Photography, hand colouring and magic image manipulation
Bernard Rosa

http:\\www.illusion-ipi.com.au

Contents

The secret way

The way to Fairyland is not as secret as most people think. You don't have to travel a long way. It may be as close as your own garden or the peaceful place you like to sit. The secret of how to get there lies within you. All you need are the three keys. Let me give you the keys.

The first key is believing in Fairies, as nothing can exist unless you believe it does. This unlocks the first door.

A pure heart and child-like mind unlocks the second door.

The third key is truly wanting to go there.

Sit quietly in your garden and you will see things you have never seen before. At first you may only see a slight movement. It could be a grasshopper disguised as a leaf, or a little lizard that you thought was a stick. Then, if you are really still, you might start to see the fairies who live there. Use the three keys now to see how many fairies you can see in the picture.

The Magic Elixir

Very early on the last day of the full moon, just before the sky turned from twilight blue to rosy pink, Fianna and her friends Peg Mouse and Bella Butterfly set out to gather the ingredients to make the magic fairy elixir. This very special potion allows humans to see the invisible fairy world.

"We have to work fast," said Fianna "to gather the dewdrops before the first golden rays of the sun dry them up."

Peg and Fianna crouched under the lowest stems of the bluebells and found the leaves laden with dewdrops that looked like sparkling crystal balls.

"Look Peg, over there is the biggest drop we have seen today. Let's pick that one." Fianna held the crystal and laughed as the drop tickled her hands. She carefully placed it in a tiny silver cup in her basket.

At last the cup was full with sparkling drops, and now it was Bella Butterfly's turn to collect the nectar from deep within the freshly opened flowers.

Peg and Fianna laughed as Bella wiggled to get out of a flower that was not quite open enough. When she finally emerged her face was covered in golden, glistening nectar. Peg wiped Bella's face clean with a soft, wet leaf. They filled a golden cup with sweet-tasting nectar and placed it in Fianna's basket.

"My turn now girls," said Fianna. "I must find the biggest and best bluebells." She fluttered her wings, flew to the very top stem of the flowers, and filled her basket with bluebells as she glided down.

"I'll race you back to the fairy ring," called Bella, when Fianna touched the ground. Fianna climbed on to Peg's back, holding the basket as tightly as she could, then Peg scurried as fast as her little white legs would take her. They arrived just as Bella gracefully alighted on a red and white spotted toadstool.

"You win Bella. Now let's begin to make the elixir," said Fianna. "You mix and I'll sing. Mix gently, five stirs in a star shape to the right and five to the left. Now for the magic spell."

Fianna scooped the golden mixture into the fresh bluebells. The three danced around and around the magic ring, singing:

> Seven drops for clear sight;
> May you only see what's right.
> Seven drops of golden nectar,
> So you'll be forever protected.
> Fairy bells give joy not sorrow,
> For those whose hearts are pure tomorrow.

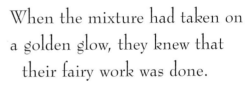

When the mixture had taken on a golden glow, they knew that their fairy work was done.

"Let's play now friends, for tonight, when the sky turns to midnight blue, I have much to do. Many of the Big People have been kind and true and I shall reward them by wetting their eyes with the magic elixir so that they may see our world and visit us in their dreams. When the veil is taken from their eyes, and as long as their hearts are pure, they will be able to see us. Imagine their surprise!"

The Golden Lantern

"Wake up Alice!" her mother called, "Time to get ready for school."

"Oh no!" cried Alice as she tumbled out of her dream and back into her bed. "It was just a dream but it seemed so real. Mummy, Mummy," she called, "I had the most wonderful dream. Can I tell you before I forget it?"

"Yes darling, we have time," said her mother as she settled down next to Alice.

"Last night as I drifted off to sleep," began Alice, "I listened to the soft music you played for me to stop me from having bad dreams. I seemed to float for a while and the next thing I remember I was lying on the grass under a huge tree. It was very dark, but I could just make out these little people peering down at me from the tree. The most beautiful one floated down and spoke.

"'Alice,' she said, 'I am Titania, Queen of the Fairies. We need your help. Our golden lantern grows dimmer each night, as the magic cocoon that lives within it is ready to hatch into a butterfly. The lantern lights the way to guide sleeping children down the hidden pathway into Dreamland. Without its glow the children will not know where to go. Will you help us?'

"'Why do you need my help?' I asked.

"'Only a child can find the golden lantern. A mortal child who is calm, kind and of pure mind is needed for the task,' explained Titania. 'We sent out a call to all children who could help, and you drifted into Fairyland on the waves of the gentle music. If you help, you will not be alone; Swift the night bird will go with you.'

"I said I would help, and immediately a small bird appeared. Then Titania waved her wand and I felt myself grow smaller and smaller, until I was the same size as the fairies. And I had the most delicate blue gossamer wings.

"Swift and I flew off into the towering mountains but found no

sign of the lantern. We glided down to the edges of a misty lake and searched the silent shores, but still found no golden lantern.

"Then, as we rested on the very top of a tree, the silver moon emerged from behind a puffy cloud, and far down in the meadow we could see a golden glimmer.

"We glided towards it and the closer we got, the brighter it became. We saw that it was a glowing cocoon, resting on a branch. I plucked the cocoon from the branch and climbed on to the night bird's back. Then we carried the precious treasure back to Fairyland.

"Titania was standing on a beautiful flower with her hands outstretched to receive the lantern. Just as I was about to give it to her you called and I woke up in my bed.

"Mummy, it was so real. Do you think I will go there again?"

"When I was a little girl I used to have the most magical dreams," answered Alice's mother, "and when I wanted to return to Fairyland I used to think about my dreams just before I dozed off to sleep. Sometimes I would pop straight back into where I left the night before. Now – it's time to get ready for school."

As Alice jumped out of bed, something blue floated to the floor. "My gossamer wings!" cried Alice. "Now I know I can go back to Fairyland whenever I want."

Moon Magic

As the full moon rose high into the midnight sky, Rozalie, the Guardian Angel of fairy children, sent a message for all the fairy children to meet her at the magic circle.

"My children," she sang in her enchanting voice, "Come to me and tell me what frightens you. I will gather your fears and send them into the sky to become the starry jewels of the night."

Lucilla, Marigold and Nub came first, closely followed by Sam, Blueboy, Buttercup, and finally Gem and Sparkle, who were so shy that they hid behind a toadstool.

When they had all gathered around, Rozalie explained to them: "Little ones, I see that you have all been frightened. If you are to help the Earth children with their fears, you must be fearless yourself. Now each of you step forward and speak of your fear and I will, with your permission and the power of the Moon, take them away."

Lucilla spoke for her brother and sister: "We were resting under the yellow tiger lilies, enjoying the warmth of the afternoon sun, when Cinder the kitten from Farmer Bill's place pounced on us. He was only playing, but he gave us such a fright that we shake with fear every time we hear a rustle in the grass, even if it is only a wee field mouse."

Sam stepped forward next, waving his golden sword. He spoke for himself and Blueboy, who was too upset to say a word. "We set out early this morning," he began in a shaky voice, "to explore the glow worm caves. We felt very brave as we marched into the cave, but the further we went the darker it became. Suddenly all the lights vanished. We could hear strange noises, and soft things

brushed our faces. We no longer felt brave and fled from the cave, and now we are afraid of the dark. Can you help us, as we want to help the children."

"Of course," said Rozalie. "Don't you know that you have to be very quiet in the caves? Your noisy chatter woke the wee fruit bats from their sleep, and scared the glow worms so much that they turned off their lights. Next time go quietly and notice how many glow worms you see."

Buttercup could hardly speak, but after a while she said, in a most melodious voice, "I feel my voice is not as beautiful as my sister's, and I am afraid to sing."

Gem and Sparkle held hands and whispered, "We are very shy and we are afraid to speak, even to our own folk. Can you help us?"

"Yes, my little friends. The most important thing is that you told me your fears. They are now as light as fairy dust, so I can gather them all in my magic cloth and send them into the midnight sky so they can become the sparkling stars. Now you are ready to help the Earth children."

the wee folk

It was the first day of spring, a day of great celebration and fun in the land of Mu. Mu can be found in the far eastern corner of Fairyland, very close to the border with Dark Corner.

The four young folk were excited, as they had been chosen to lead the parade to the stone door where Opal the wise one would tell the tale of the war of the Hairy Trolls.

Aaron was the most excited of the Wee Folk as he was to ride the grey squirrel and carry the crystal staff. Of all the treasures in Mu, the crystal staff was the most precious. It had the power to make trees grow where there were none, to turn an ugly toad into a handsome young prince, or to produce food for a great feast. In fact, it could do anything the bearer wished.

From far and wide the Wee Folk came bearing gifts of large brown nuts. Furry grey squirrels scurried from every tree and followed the proud bearer of the crystal staff. They marched through the cool dark forest, up the winding path to the huge oak tree that hid the cracked stone door that marked the entrance to Middle Kingdom.

There was much talking and laughing as folk who had not seen each other for a full year arrived.

They were all young and bold, for no one grew old in the land of Mu. They only grew wise.

Opal called "Quiet everyone. Once I have told the tale there will be plenty of time for celebration and feasting."

At the mention of feasting the gathering stilled, as the Wee Folk liked nothing better than a good feast.

Opal cleared his throat and began in his low rumbling voice. "Many years ago, about two hundred years after the beginning of time, our land was rich and green, just as it is today. Life was wonderful for us Wee Folk. The sun always shone, food was abundant and we knew nothing about fighting or war.

"Everyone was a friend – or so we thought. Little did we know that in the earth below our very feet, the Hairy Trolls were planning to invade us and take our crystal staff. They were an untidy and angry tribe who had destroyed their land and wanted ours. For many weeks they had been gathering, and one day in late summer, when they knew we would be relaxing after a very scrumptious feast, they struck.

"The earth started to tremble and the rocks began to roll, and then hundreds of red-eyed Hairy Trolls burst through the stone door and took the crystal staff. We ran and hid and would have been driven from our land if it hadn't been for our squirrel friends. They came to our aid and hunted those nasty trolls, biting at their heels with sharp teeth and throwing nuts at them from the treetops. They battled many a long day, until they finally drove the last screaming troll back through the broken door.

"When the deed was done they sealed it tight and planted this great oak tree so the trolls could never pass this way again.

"We celebrated long into the night, drinking only the best blackberry wine and eating cheese and bread, just as we will do this very night. So bring forward the nuts you have gathered as a token of thanks for the brave deeds done by our squirrel friends."

The Wee Folk cheered at the end of the tale that they loved and knew so well.

Now it was Aaron's turn to speak, for as the bearer of the crystal staff it was his duty to wish the food for the feast.

"Magic crystal," shouted Aaron in a voice loud enough for all to hear. "I wish for apple pie and ice cream, crisp bread and fresh cheese, and of course the best blackberry wine."

Everyone cheered as Aaron cried: "Let the feast begin!"

25

Quiet Magic

Georgia loved to visit her grandfather. She called him Grandpa Twinkle because his beautiful midnight blue eyes twinkled as though they had stars in them.

Grandpa Twinkle was very special because he was the only adult that Georgia knew who not only spoke about fairies, but could actually see them. She always asked, "Grandpa, why can't I see the fairies in your garden?"

His reply was always the same: "Young lady, you will see them when you truly believe in them. Fairy folk don't show themselves to just anyone. Why, the last time my favourite fairy Pammy did that, young Tom next door caught her in a jar, and it took a lot of talking and nearly a whole bag of my best lollies to get her back."

Georgia thought about his words and decided there and then that she truly believed not only in fairies, but also in the stories her Grandpa told her. For in her whole life she had never met another person who knew just what she was thinking and who made her feel important. She wanted to know his secret and have that feeling always, not just when she was with Grandpa Twinkle.

"Ted," she said to her much-loved teddy bear, "let's see if we can find the fairies." She started searching with Ted, looking under leaves and peering into the middle of flowers, and everywhere else her Grandpa told her fairies lived. But she didn't see a trace of them, not even a wing.

Then she remembered another very important thing her Grandpa had told her. "You must sit very, very quietly. Close your eyes, and still all those thoughts that are chasing each other in your head. Fairies can see, feel and hear thoughts, and they only come out when they feel it is truly safe, and when your mind is quiet and still like a pond."

Georgia sat down with Ted and leaned against the old oak tree that Grandpa loved. She tried to be quiet, but her mind was very busy. She thought about her breakfast, the clothes she wore to school, the homework she had to do and the TV show she had watched the night before.

Georgia tried harder and harder until all the thoughts ran away. She felt a quietness creeping in, and her mind became still and quiet.

Just then she felt a tingle and a flutter on her hand and heard a tinkling laugh. She opened her eyes and at first thought she had imagined it, but then from behind her a tiny voice said, "Hey, can't you see us? We are down here."

Georgia stood up and peered around the tree. There to her amazement stood two tiny fairies; the tree she was leaning against was their home. She rubbed her eyes and blinked a few times, but the fairies were still there.

"You are real," she said, whispering in case she scared them away. "You are just like Grandpa told me. Why – you are Pammy and you must be Misty Blue. I am Georgia. Can I play with you?"

Pammy and Misty Blue both laughed and said, "Of course. We have been wanting to play with you for so long, but you couldn't see us."

Georgia and Ted spent a magical afternoon playing with their new friends and eating delicious fairy cake. When it was time to leave, Georgia promised that she would come back often and sit quietly until her friends joined her.

Lily Lizard

Adam was very excited when he was awoken at dawn on the first day of May: today he was to start his training as a Guardian of the Land. Adam had been chosen from all his fairy friends to look after every living thing in the forest.

He hurried to dress, and ran out of the mossy green mound where he lived with his family. He expected to see his teacher waiting for him, but all he saw was a scaly brown lizard lying very still, basking in the early morning sun.

Adam waited and waited, thinking that, at any minute, one of the wise Spirit Elves would appear. Finally he turned to the lizard and asked, "Have you seen my teacher?"

"Why yes," replied the lizard. "I am your teacher. Let me introduce myself. I am Lily."

Adam was shocked. "What can this scaly old lizard know about the forest that I don't already know?" he thought.

Suddenly Lily whispered, "Be still and quiet lad, it's time for my breakfast."

Adam stood very still for what seemed like hours to a young fairy who was used to racing through the forest with his friends.

Suddenly a fly landed on Lily's nose. Adam dared not move in case the fly saw him and flew away. In a flash, out flicked Lily's red tongue, and the fly seemed to vanish before his eyes.

"Yum," said Lily. "Did you see that, lad? The fly couldn't see me because I became part of the land around me. Now I've had breakfast we can start work."

Adam thought he had already done his day's work, as he found it very tiring standing still.

They walked through the forest and talked and talked. They met many creatures on their walk, and Lily knew them all. She introduced Adam to them by saying, "I would like you to meet young Adam. He has been honoured by being chosen as a Guardian of the Forest. So when he has finished his training, if you have any problems, go and see him. He lives under the mossy mound."

Adam felt very proud, and as they talked he began to like Lily a little bit more.

Sometimes they would stay very still and quiet while Lily pointed out many things that Adam couldn't see at first. She would whisper, "Be still lad," and then a tiny green tree frog or a beautiful furry caterpillar would appear from nowhere. Once they watched a butterfly shed its dull cocoon and transform itself into one of the most beautiful beings in the forest.

Adam had never seen so much life in the forest before. Much to his surprise he began to enjoy himself, and was sorry when Lily said, "That's it for today lad, I will see you at the same time tomorrow. Go to bed early, as we are walking all the way to the pond tomorrow, and I have a lot to teach you. The most important lesson you learnt today was that in stillness, all you want will come to you."

Lily walked over to a pile of leaves and, with a flick of her tail, she disappeared. Adam blinked his eyes and there she was again. "Hello and goodbye again," said Lily. "I will teach you how to do that one day soon."

Water Baby

As the first rays of the golden sun sparkled on the still water of the Blue Lake, Mia happily rose from the fairy world beneath the cool water. She looked eagerly to see if Mirabu was there to greet her, but he was nowhere to be seen. While she waited she remembered the day many years ago when she had first found the tiny babe she named Mirabu.

She had been sitting by the lake singing with her bird friends, when she heard a strange sound like a young cub crying. She thought it might have been a wolf cub who had fallen in the lake, so she went to see if she could help. To her surprise it wasn't a furry cub but a tiny human baby on a lily pad.

As she cradled the baby in her arms for the first time, she looked into his innocent dark eyes and fell in love with him. She named the human child Mirabu, which in fairy words means miracle child.

During the days she sang to him and found sweet food for him to eat, but when the moon rose into the sky, she had to return to her watery home. Then she would leave him in a warm cave in the care of the night birds. For many months Mirabu slept soundly through the night. But there came a day when he began to crawl and woke before dawn to explore the shore of the lake on his own. Mia knew she had to find a kind human to watch over him in the night.

Close by lived a noble tribe who knew of the water fairy and her human child. They were happy to care for the young child, who knew more about the forest than even their wise chief. For during Mirabu's long and happy days with Mia he had learnt the magic ways of the fairies and could talk to the animals and trees.

Every day until his tenth year, Mirabu was always by the lake at dawn, waiting for his tiny winged mother. Some mornings he could be found with his face touching the water, watching for the first bubbles to signal her arrival. He would laugh with delight as she shook the water from her hair in a crystal shower. Other days he would hide under a pile of leaves or high in a tree. Mirabu thought he was very clever tricking his mother, but she only pretended she couldn't see him; she always knew where he was.

Each day was an adventure. Sometimes they would visit the eagles high in the mountains or ride the gentle deer deep into the woods. But their happiest days were spent at the lake. Mia taught Mirabu how to dive deep into the water, but no matter how hard he tried he could never go as deep as she could. He longed to visit Mia's home and meet the other water fairies she told him about.

Lately Mirabu had been arriving late, or sometimes not at all, and Mia was sad as she thought that he may be planning to live with his own kind. Mirabu had no such plans. Just as Mia was about to return to the lake, she heard a low soft whistle that signaled Mirabu's arrival. He came towards her with a wide grin on his face, took hold of her little hand and dived deep into the water with her. He had been secretly practising his diving, and this very day he had been able to stay on the bottom of the lake for a long long time.

Now Mirabu could join Mia and her family whenever he liked, deep in the water of the Blue Lake.

The Queen's Birthday

Have you received an invitation to Queen Titania's birthday party?" asked Danielle.

"Of course," replied Josh. "Everyone is invited, even the grumpy old toad from the pond. It's going to be so much fun. The food is always so delicious at parties. I especially love the cake and fizzy dewdrops."

"My favourites are honeysuckle juice, jam tarts and chocolate pudding. It makes me happy just thinking about them," cried Danielle, licking her lips.

"It is going to be a grand night, but what are you giving Titania for her birthday?" asked Josh.

"I thought I would make her a new wand, with a sparkling crystal at the end, magical enough to turn even the grumpy toad into a handsome prince."

Josh laughed, "You can't do that, you have to know an awful lot of spells. Why, you would have to do at least another five years at school before you were that powerful."

"Do you have any suggestions then?" asked Danielle.

"If you would like to help, we could give her a new cloak. We could make it from the finest spiders' silk, with buttons of sparkling crystal. She would look so beautiful, and it would keep her warm and dry. Spiders' silk is so strong that you can't break it, and water can't go through it either."

"Oh yes!" exclaimed Danielle. "That would be the best present. No one else would think of making her a new cloak. But where will we find the finest spiders' silk?"

"Well, let me think," said Josh. "Andrew Spider lives in the cave on the top of Misty Mountain. Maybe he will spin us some silk. Or there is Simo Spider from under the log."

"No, neither of those will do," replied Danielle. "Andrew Spider

lives too far away, and Simo Spider is annoyed with me because I untangled Molly Ladybird from his web."

They were both sitting there quietly thinking, when they heard a whisper: "What about me?"

"Who said that?" they both asked at the same time.

"I did. Look behind you," said Black Spider, who had been listening the whole time. "I also received an invitation to the party and was wondering what to give Titania. I spin the finest silk. Just look at my web down there. Isn't it beautiful? That is the best you will find. If I spin the silk, you can weave the cloak and find the crystals. Then the three of us can give it to her."

"That's wonderful", said Danielle as she clapped her hands with joy. Then she became very quiet as she remembered what her grandmother had told her just the other day.

"Danielle," she had said, "I have been given sparkling wands and pots of gold, but the gifts I have cherished most have been made by the people I love and who love me. The lemon drops you made me the other day were the best gift I have had in a long time. I enjoyed every single one of them."

"I know the queen will like our present, because we are making it ourselves and we are doing it with love," said Danielle. "Let's get started."

The Shadow Fairy

Gigi was an exceptional little fairy. At an age when most fairies are still chasing butterflies and playing hide-and-seek in the meadows with their friends, Gigi was made the guardian of the beautiful old mulberry grove.

She loved to lie on the huge leaves of the mulberry trees, listening to her grandmother telling tales of long ago as she gathered the glistening threads of the silk worm to weave into special gowns for the Fairy Queen.

The majestic trees also whispered tales to her, of the times before her people journeyed from beyond the North Star. As she listened to their wisdom, her love of the great trees grew.

The mulberry grove grew deep within the forest, and in the past had rarely been disturbed by the outside world. But lately, the Big People had been venturing further and further into the forest. Gigi saw that they were not as caring of the trees as the fairy folk. They damaged and cut the branches of the great trees to make campfires.

Sometimes when they left, they didn't put out their fires properly. And their rubbish littered the forest floor beneath the old trees.

Each night, before she wrapped herself in a soft new leaf to sleep, Gigi sang songs of healing to the trees. Each day she woke before dawn to make sure the fires had been put out.

More and more of the Big People came, and Gigi spent more and more of her time working with the great trees, until one night she dared not close her eyes. The Big People and their children were having fun under the canopy of the trees, but Gigi trembled when she saw them light their fires as darkness fell. She was afraid to sleep in case these careless people set the whole forest alight.

Gigi's eyes were nearly closing when she heard a spark fly out of the fire and into the dry leaves. Soon the leaves were burning and the fire was beginning to spread. She needed help to put out the fire, and the only way she could think of to alert everyone was to ring the crystal bell.

The bell was only used on occasions of great importance, such as announcing the arrival of folk from distant parts of the land. Everyone came running, wondering what all the excitement was about. As soon as they saw the fire, they swung into action. Poppy the rainmaker called in the clouds, the gnomes used their shovels to throw dirt on the flames and the fairy folk used their magic to gather large stones to halt the spread of the fire. Very soon the fire was under control and everyone agreed that Gigi had saved their homes.

As a reward for her unselfish love of the trees, the Fairy Queen gave Gigi a gift of a Fairy Shadow. This meant that while she slept, her shadow could keep watch over the forest. Gigi could now spend her days repairing the forest.

At night, while the little children slept under the trees, she entered their dreams and spoke to them of her beloved forest while her shadow watched over the trees. She showed them all the little creatures that made the forest their home, and told them how much they relied on people to care for their land.

Very soon all the forest folk noticed that the Big People had changed. They only used dead wood for their fires, and made sure they put them out properly. Best of all, when they left, they took all their rubbish with them. What a difference one little fairy managed to make to the forest.

fairies of the seasons

Tim's eyes became very sleepy as the elephant-shaped cloud disappeared behind the tall tree. He had spent many afternoons lying beneath the towering oak trees with his cousin Ben, playing their favourite game of seeing who could find the most shapes in the clouds. But today Tim was on his own, and as he lay quietly he was lulled into a deep sleep by the bird song and the warm autumn sun.

Slowly he became aware of a very soft and gentle sound, like wind chimes, but there were no chimes in the woods. He thought that perhaps he was dreaming. But a strong gust of wind made the crinkly golden leaves swirl around his head. Then he knew that he was awake and that he could still hear the musical chimes.

At first he thought the music was coming from behind the tree, but just as he moved towards it, it changed direction and seemed to come from down the path.

"I know," he thought. "Ben is hiding in the trees and playing a joke on me. I will catch him."

He very slowly and quietly crept towards the sound, and slowly parted the leaves of the tree. There was no sign of Ben, but as he looked more carefully, he saw three tiny fairies with long golden hair. They looked at him and laughed. "Close your mouth Tim, you may swallow a fly if you're not careful," said one of the fairies.

"Are you real?" cried Tim.

Again they laughed. "Of course we are real. We are the fairies of the seasons and we let the trees know when it is time to sleep and to wake. My name is Melody and this is Harmony and Jade. It is time for the trees to prepare for the coming of winter. We are playing them music to make their thoughts long, deep and slow, until they nod off into their winter sleep and dream the dream of new life. If we hadn't called the wind and sent it after you, you too would have fallen under our spell and slept until we came to play the music of spring."

"Trees don't think!" replied Tim indignantly. "They just stay where they are planted, and grow."

"Tim, you have a lot to learn," said Melody. "Haven't you heard their soft whispers as you have laid beneath them? The reason you heard us today was because you were so quiet. Listen harder next time and you will hear the trees."

"Watch the trees while we play," said Jade. "You will see for yourself how they let go of their leaves and curl their soft green stems and gently nod."

The three began to play the most beautiful music, and Tim found it hard to stay awake as he watched the rain of soft leaves swirl to the ground while all around him the tall trees began to slowly nod.

He listened to his new friends' music until the sun began to sink behind the mountains and it was time to go home. As he turned to leave, Jade said: "Come back in spring Tim, when we play the music of new life, and then you can watch the trees wake up and stretch their limbs and unroll their soft new leaves."

"You are right," said Tim. "Trees do think. I have watched them sway and nod to your beautiful music. When I come back in spring, can I bring my cousin Ben?"

"We will be waiting for you both," replied Melody. "Don't be late as the trees are impatient to stretch after their long deep sleep."

The Silver Shell

Tessa, Sam, and Pip Fairy were on the beach looking for a special seashell, when they heard someone laughing. As quick as a blink, they made themselves invisible, as fairies don't like to be seen by just anyone.

"Who is it?" whispered Pip.

"I don't know," replied Sam.

"It's me, Mig," answered a laughing voice. "I'm over here, in the water."

They all turned around and saw a small creature waving at them from the water. They looked closer, and to their amazement realised the creature was a merboy. Their parents had told them about mermaids, but they had never seen one.

"Can you still see us?" they cried. "We should be invisible."

"Of course," answered Mig. "But what are you? You look like the Big People but you are smaller and have wings like my bird friends. What are your names?"

"I am Pip and this is my sister Tessa and brother Sam," answered Pip. "We are fairies and we live in the Enchanted Forest. We came in search of a special seashell for our mother's birthday, but there don't seem to be any here."

"No, you won't find many on the beach any more because when the humans come they take them. Sometimes they take the shells my friends live in, and I never see them again. However, I know a cave at the bottom of the ocean where there are lots of shells. I'll take you there."

"We have never been to the bottom of the ocean. Do you think we can swim that far?" asked Sam.

"I will help you," answered Mig.

With Mig in the lead, the strange group set off to explore the ocean floor. They swam through a great forest of waving seaweed, past fish and strange creatures of all shapes, sizes and colours, and dived deeper and deeper until they reached the cave.

There were so many beautiful shells to choose from. But in a dark corner of the cave a silver glow led them to the prettiest shell they had ever seen. Its silver curves sparkled with all the colours of the rainbow. This was the shell for their mother. Tessa cradled the shell in her arms as they followed Mig back to the surface.

The fairies wanted Mig to see their home, but he couldn't fly and was too heavy for them to carry. Suzy the seagull was sunning herself next to them and overheard their conversation.

"If you hold tight to my legs," she said, "I will take you. I have always wanted to visit the Enchanted Forest."

Mig held very very tight at first, because he was scared – he had never been above the ocean waves before. But he soon forgot his fear and cried with joy: "Suzy, take me higher and higher. I want to touch the sky. I love to fly!"

The three fairies led the way to the Enchanted Forest, holding the precious shell between them.

What excitement they created when they arrived with their strange new friend. They hid the shell behind their backs so that they could surprise their mother with its beauty.

"Happy birthday!" they all shouted at once, as they gave the shell to their mother. "But what happened to our shell?" cried Pip. "It was silvery and beautiful when it was in the water. Now it's just grey."

Their mother laughed as she looked at their puzzled faces. "The sea gives the shell its glow," she said. "So now we will all have to visit Mig at his home so that I can see its beauty. Won't that be fun?"

They happily flew with Mig and the shell back to the beach, and as they waved good-bye, they promised to return with their mother very soon.

robin's Nest

For many days the Robins had been taking turns sitting on their beautiful speckled eggs. Mrs Robin was concerned that if they left it much longer, they may not have time to gather the soft moss they needed to line the nest before the eggs began to hatch.

"Red Robin," said Mrs Robin to her husband, "we will both have to go to the crystal waterfall soon to gather the moss."

"Yes, Sweet," replied Red Robin, "but I am afraid we can't leave our eggs without having someone to watch them. There have been some strange happenings in the forest lately. Why, only yesterday two eggs went missing from Penny Pigeon's nest."

Little did they know that the Devas, who are the nature spirits that live in every tree, had been listening and felt sorry for them.

"If the Robins do not get the moss the little chicks will be very uncomfortable and will squawk all night," said Leila, who lived in the leaf closest to the nest.

"That happened last spring with the sparrows," complained Seine. "Their nest wasn't lined because they were waiting until the last moment so the moss would be fresh and soft. The chicks hatched five days early and they squawked from one meal to the next."

"Who shall we ask to egg sit?" said Leila. "Maybe Sweet Sparrow," replied Jewel.

"She has a nest of eggs herself," said Leila. "I know, let's invite the Song Fairies. They are such fun, and I love their singing."

So they asked Blue Butterfly, who happened to be visiting their tree at that moment, to take a message to the fairies.

Before you could blink the fairies arrived and began to sing.

"O Red Robins, go and play.
For all this day we will stay.
It will be our turn to say good-bye
When the golden sun leaves the sky,
Return when the moon rises into the night.
Have no worry, everything will be all right."

"Thank you, thank you little friends," sang the Robins as they flew off for a day of gathering moss and playing at the crystal falls.

The Song Fairies – Bell, Gai and Rose – gathered around the nest to keep the eggs warm, and all morning sang songs of the forest to the speckled eggs. At noon Thorrin the elf arrived with his magic fiddle and joined the fairies in their song. The music was so enchanting that even the leaf devas, who are usually very shy and always careful not to be seen, showed their beautiful faces and added their voices to the chorus.

Soon the whole forest joined in song, and in what seemed liked minutes the silver moon rose into the starry sky.

The Robins could hear the magical choir as they returned happy and refreshed from their day at the waterfall. They joined in the song with their sweet piping voices.

"I'll get dinner while you line the nest," offered Mr Robin.

Just as Mrs Robin tucked the last piece of moss into place, the speckled eggs began to crack. Very soon five new squawking voices joined in the night song.

free Spirit

All across Fairyland, the fairies were celebrating the birth of Tarashar, the first-born daughter of the Fairy King and Queen. Every fairy who could do so attended the future queen's birth, and bestowed the most wonderful gifts and virtues upon her.

Helena, who lived beyond the Westwind, gave her the last and strangest gift.

"Nature child," she said, "I give you the gift of Free Spirit."

All those present were puzzled, and whispered to each other, "What does she mean by Free Spirit?"

From the beginning, Tarashar was very different from any other royal fairy they could remember. Her wings were not like those of other royal fairies – long, graceful and splashed with silver and gold – but were small and multi-coloured like the flowers of the meadow. And she preferred the song of the birds to the sweet lullabies her mother sang.

Tarashar's mother tried to dress her in the beautiful flowing clothes and delicate shoes befitting of a royal fairy, but she had them off before the last ribbon was tied.

Just before her tenth birthday, Tarashar's mother asked what special present she would like.

"Mother," she pleaded, "my only wish is for some clothes just like my elf friends wear. When I play with the elves my lovely dresses get caught in the leaves and branches of the trees and I always get left behind."

The morning of her birthday soon arrived, and when Tarashar opened her eyes the first things she saw were the forest-green elf clothes laid out on her bed. Quick as a flash she put them on and flew out of the window to join the birds and animals who had started gathering at dawn to greet her.

Her happy laugh could be heard all over the kingdom as she raced the furry spotted caterpillars with the elf children.

As the time approached to begin her royal training, Tarashar's parents and teachers tried to tame her boisterous spirit. She would politely listen to them before racing outside to help an injured animal or climb a tree. Sometimes they would find her singing songs of nature into the ear of any big person who was fortunate enough to venture into the Enchanted Forest.

Everything is done with love and a light heart in the fairy kingdom, so Tarashar's parents could not be angry with her. Tarashar was a loving, kind and gentle fairy. But eventually, when patience and love had not tamed her, her parents called in the wise ones to help them.

These ancient, wise fairies read the books of fairy history to see if they could find an answer, locking themselves away for days and days. When everyone had nearly given up hope, the wise ones finally emerged.

They told her astonished parents, and all the fairies who had come to listen, that Tarashar's great-great-great-grandmother, after whom she had been named, had been blessed with the same free spirit as Tarashar. Her parents too had allowed her the freedom to be herself. She had become a grand queen who ventured further from the fairy realm than anyone else before her. She restored desolate lands to their former beauty and brought the many peoples of Fairyland together.

Now Tarashar's parents knew that the destiny of their beautiful nature child was to become a great queen. They understood the wonderful gift of her free spirit and allowed her to roam the forest and play with the elves, learning about the land and the many different creatures in Fairyland. She truly was a free spirit.

Bernard Rosa

Bernard Rosa was born on January 18th 1961 in Canberrra Australia. Bondi has been his home for the last ten years. From an early age he showed great artistic ability, but it wasn't until 1990 that he turned this talent into a career. Although he has no formal training as a photographer, he was successful from the beginning, with exhibitions in Sydney, San Francisco and Los Angeles. He has explored and mastered many different styles of photography but for the moment has settled on bringing the mystical to life in the form of black and white computer enhanced images of Fairies, Mermaids and Angels. This is his fourth book in the series. Bernard enjoys working with children and endeavours to bring fantasy and imagination into his work to stimulate the minds of young and old alike. His unique style of photography and portrayal of mystical images is fast becoming recognised internationally.

Sleep, deep sleep in peace.
Travel to far away places.
i will watch and keep you safe
until we again trade places.

Published in Australia by
New Holland Publishers (Australia) Pty Ltd
Sydney • Auckland • London • Cape Town

14 Aquatic Drive Frenchs Forest NSW 2086 Australia
218 Lake Road Northcote Auckland New Zealand
86 Edgware Road London W2 2EA United Kingdom
80 McKenzie Street Cape Town 8001 South Africa

Copyright © 1998 in text: Janine Fuller
Copyright © 1998 in images: Bernard Rosa
Copyright © 2002 New Holland Publishers (Australia) Pty Ltd

The moral rights of the author have been asserted.

First published in 1998 by Hodder Moa Beckett Publishers Limited
[a member of the Hodder Headline Group]
This edition published in 2002 by New Holland Publishers (Australia) Pty Ltd

ISBN 1 74110 014 3

All rights reserved. No part of this publication may be reproduced, stored in a retrieval system
or transmitted, in any form or by any means, electronic, mechanical, photocopying, recording
or otherwise, without the prior written permission of the publishers and copyright holders.

4 6 8 10 9 7 5 3

A CiP record of this book is available from the National Library of Australia

Publishing Manager: Anouska Good
Designer: Janine Fuller
Colour separations by Microdot, Auckland, New Zealand
Produced by Imago Services, China